P9-BHV-267

Dear Parent:

Congratulations! Your child is taking the first steps on an exciting journey. The destination? Independent reading!

STEP INTO READING® will help your child get there. The program offers five steps to reading success. Each step includes fun stories and colorful art. There are also Step into Reading Sticker Books, Step into Reading Math Readers, Step into Reading Write-In Readers, Step into Reading Phonics Readers, and Step into Reading Phonics First Steps! Boxed Sets—a complete literacy program with something for every child.

Learning to Read, Step by Step!

Ready to Read   Preschool–Kindergarten
• big type and easy words • rhyme and rhythm • picture clues
For children who know the alphabet and are eager to begin reading.

Reading with Help   Preschool–Grade 1
• basic vocabulary • short sentences • simple stories
For children who recognize familiar words and sound out new words with help.

Reading on Your Own   Grades 1–3
• engaging characters • easy-to-follow plots • popular topics
For children who are ready to read on their own.

Reading Paragraphs   Grades 2–3
• challenging vocabulary • short paragraphs • exciting stories
For newly independent readers who read simple sentences with confidence.

Ready for Chapters   Grades 2–4
• chapters • longer paragraphs • full-color art
For children who want to take the plunge into chapter books but still like colorful pictures.

STEP INTO READING® is designed to give every child a successful reading experience. The grade levels are only guides. Children can progress through the steps at their own speed, developing confidence in their reading, no matter what their grade.

Remember, a lifetime love of reading starts with a single step!

For Ramona and Leo

Copyright © 2008 Disney Enterprises, Inc. All rights reserved. Published in the United States by Random House Children's Books, a division of Random House, Inc., 1745 Broadway, New York, NY 10019, and in Canada by Random House of Canada Limited, Toronto, in conjunction with Disney Enterprises, Inc.

Step into Reading, Random House, and the Random House colophon are registered trademarks of Random House, Inc.

Visit us on the Web!
www.stepintoreading.com
www.randomhouse.com/kids/disney

Educators and librarians, for a variety of teaching tools, visit us at
www.randomhouse.com/teachers

Library of Congress Cataloging-in-Publication Data
Jordan, Apple.
My hero / by Apple Jordan ; illustrated by the Disney Storybook Artists
— 1st ed.
    p. cm. — (Step into reading. A Step 2 book.)
Summary: Bolt the dog and Penny, his master, star in a television show as heroes, with Bolt always keeping the bad guys away from Penny, but Bolt does not understand that what happens on their show is only acting.
ISBN 978-0-375-84812-4 (trade)
ISBN 978-0-375-94812-1 (lib. bdg.)
[1. Dogs—Fiction. 2. Actors and actresses—Fiction. 3. Acting—Fiction. 4. Heroes—Fiction.]
I. Disney Storybook Artists. II. Title.
PZ7.J755My 2008   [E]—dc22   2008014927

Printed in the United States of America   16 15 14   First Edition

MY HERO

WITHDRAWN

By Apple Jordan

Illustrated by Andrew Phillipson and
Jean-Paul Orpiñas and the Disney
Storybook Artists

Random House 🏠 New York

Penny found Bolt
in a pet shop.
It was love
at first sight.

"You're my good boy,"
she said.

Bolt loved Penny, too.

Penny and Bolt played heroes on a TV show. Bolt kept Penny safe from the bad guys.

Bolt could stop cars,
bark louder
than thunder,
and run super fast!

The TV show
ended each day.
But Bolt kept looking
for the bad guys.

Bolt's adventures with Penny seemed real to him!

One day, Bolt tried
to save Penny.
He ran into a window
and fell into a big box.
He got shipped
across the country!

Bolt met a cat
named Mittens.

"Where is Penny?"
Bolt cried.

Bolt found a truck
headed for home.
Mittens did not want
to go with him.

When they got hungry,
Mittens showed Bolt
how to beg for food.

Bolt and Mittens met
a hamster named Rhino.
He had seen Bolt on TV.

Bolt was Rhino's hero!

The three friends
jumped onto a train.
Bolt needed
to get home.

Along the way,
Bolt learned
how to
fetch a stick . . .

how to bury a bone . . .

and how to play
with water!

Bolt loved acting like
a regular dog.
But he still missed
Penny.

25

At last, Bolt found
the TV studio.
He started searching
for Penny.

A building was on fire.
Penny was in danger!
Bolt and his friends
raced to help.

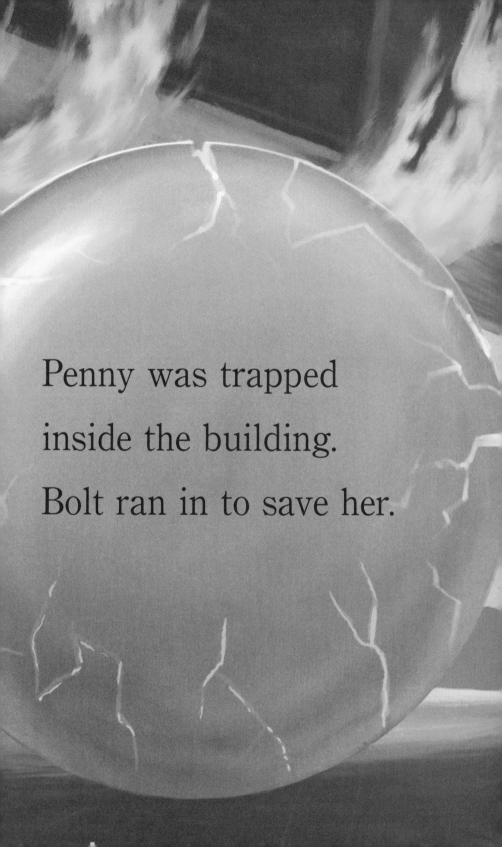

Penny was trapped inside the building.
Bolt ran in to save her.

Bolt barked loudly
into an air vent.
Firefighters came
to the rescue.

Bolt had saved Penny!

He <u>was</u> a hero!

And best of all,

he was <u>her</u> hero!